This book belongs to _____

Use the cape to draw in a picture of your mom.

My mom is a super mom!

SUPERMOM!!!

By Supermom's son

Illustrated by Danko Herrera

Copyright © 2021 by Glen Cunningham

All rights reserved.

This is a work of fiction. Any resemblance to actual events or persons, living or dead, is entirely coincidental.

Print ISBN: 978-1-7774871-2-6

eBook ISBN: 978-1-7774871-1-9

Author's email for questions/comments: SonofSupermom@gmail.com

Supermombook.com

In memory of my own super mom (Mary Joan Lawlor) who provided me with so much love, care, and help, plus a super sense of humour and imagination.

To all of the super ladies who continue to save our days without any capes or super powers!

Special Thanks:

Dan Ebbs who mentored, inspired, and encouraged me to write this endeavour. My super family and friends who supported me every step of the way. Kim Rice at Indie Publishing Group who made me feel like I was her most important client. Danko Herrera for his patience with me and who included every last detail in his illustrations.

"Aaaaaaa!" screamed Marie O'Herrow as the electricity zapped and tingled through her body.

"Mom, Mom, are you okay?" cried her son Glen.

"Wow, talk about a super shock! Yes, I'm okay. I just need to sit down and catch my breath." said Marie as she touched her electrified, curly hair.

"Here dear, have some of my homemade tea to help get back your strength." urged Grandma O'Herrow.

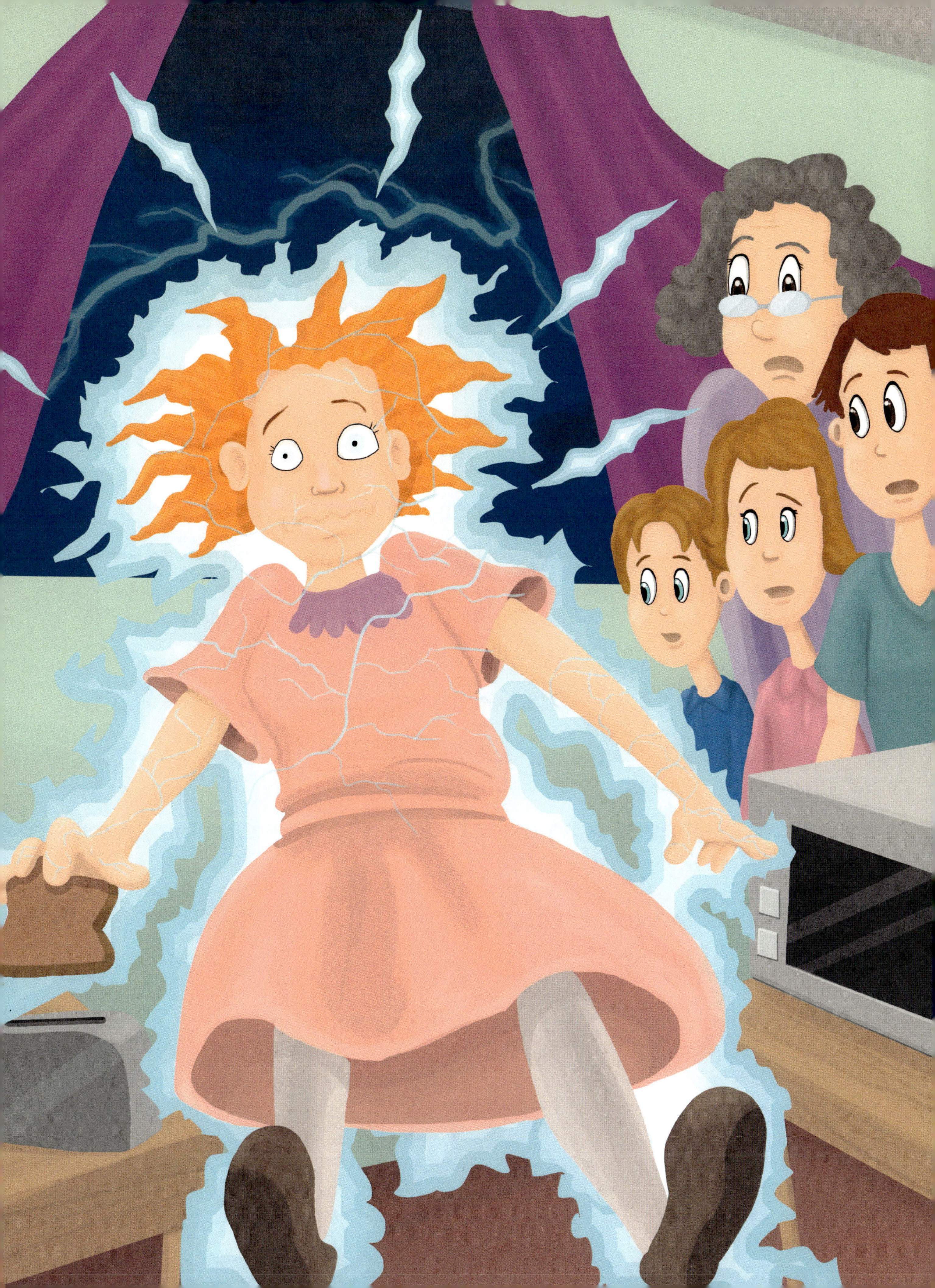

Marie took a sip of tea, and her family couldn't believe what started to happen! She sprung into the air and her body began to transform - like the Incredible Hulk but without the green skin and grumpy attitude.

"Ummm, how are you feeling, Mom?" asked her son Keith as he rubbed his eyes in disbelief.

"I have never felt better in my whole life!"

"Are you sure, dear? You just had a big accident, and you look a lot different!"

"I do?"

"Yeah! You're taller and even and more muscular than Keith!" exclaimed Glen.

"Plus, your eyes aren't blue anymore…they look more like … all the colours." Angie stated as she gazed at her mom's eyes.

"Yeah, sort of like a rainbow."

"You are all pulling my leg!"

"No mom, we're not! Go check in the mirror."

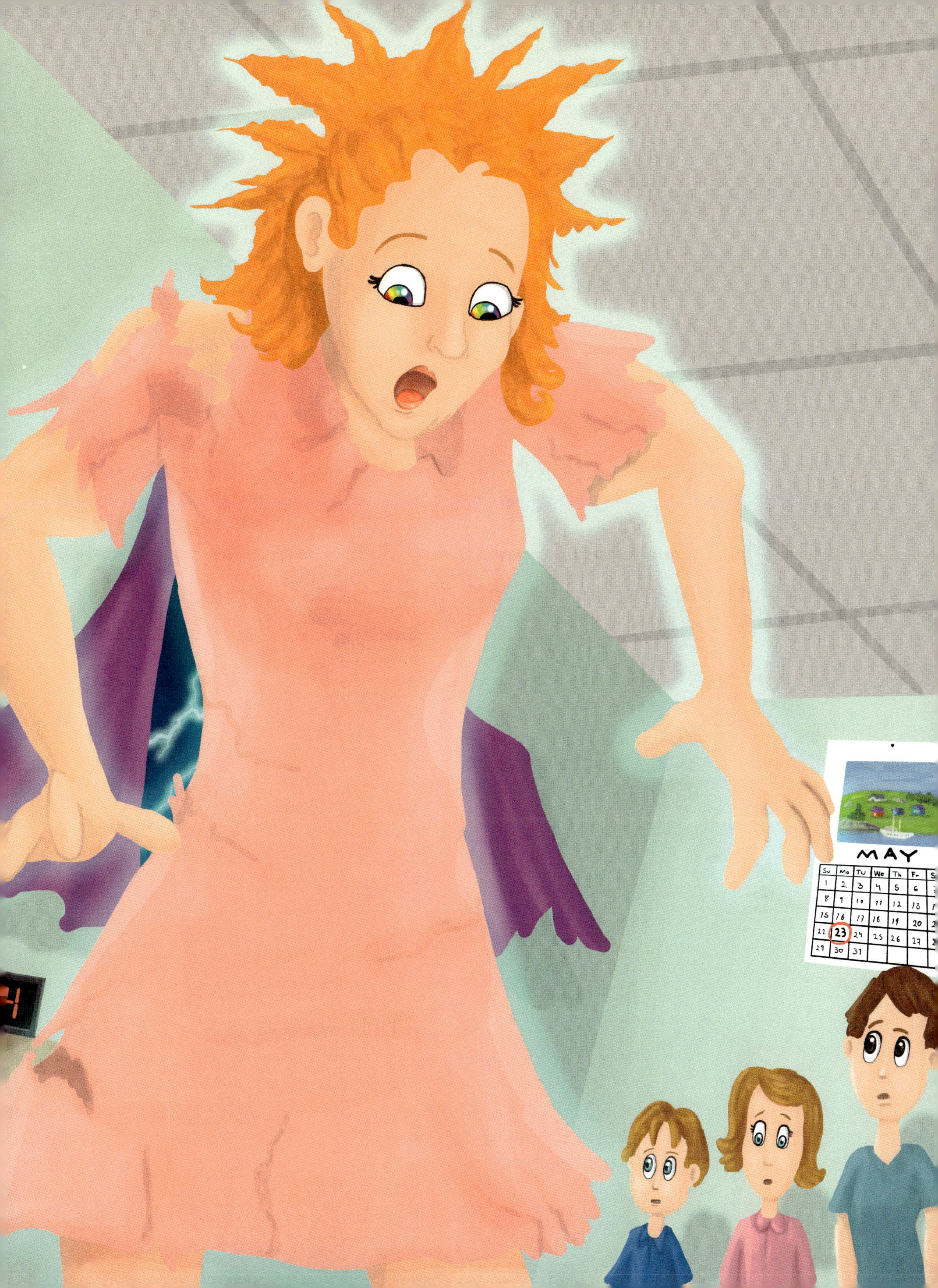
MAY

Marie decided to go along with their joke and walked over to the mirror. She froze after seeing her reflection.

"Yikes! You're right. I am much taller and muscular, plus my eyes do look like rainbows!"

"Mom! It must have been the shock from the electricity when you tried to unplug both the toaster and microwave as the lightning struck the house," shouted Glen.

"I definitely felt something run through my whole body."

"But dear, you said you never felt better. Are you super sure?" asked Grandma.

"Yes, I'm super, super sure! Except, I do have this incredible urge to build something in the garage out of our broken electric broom."

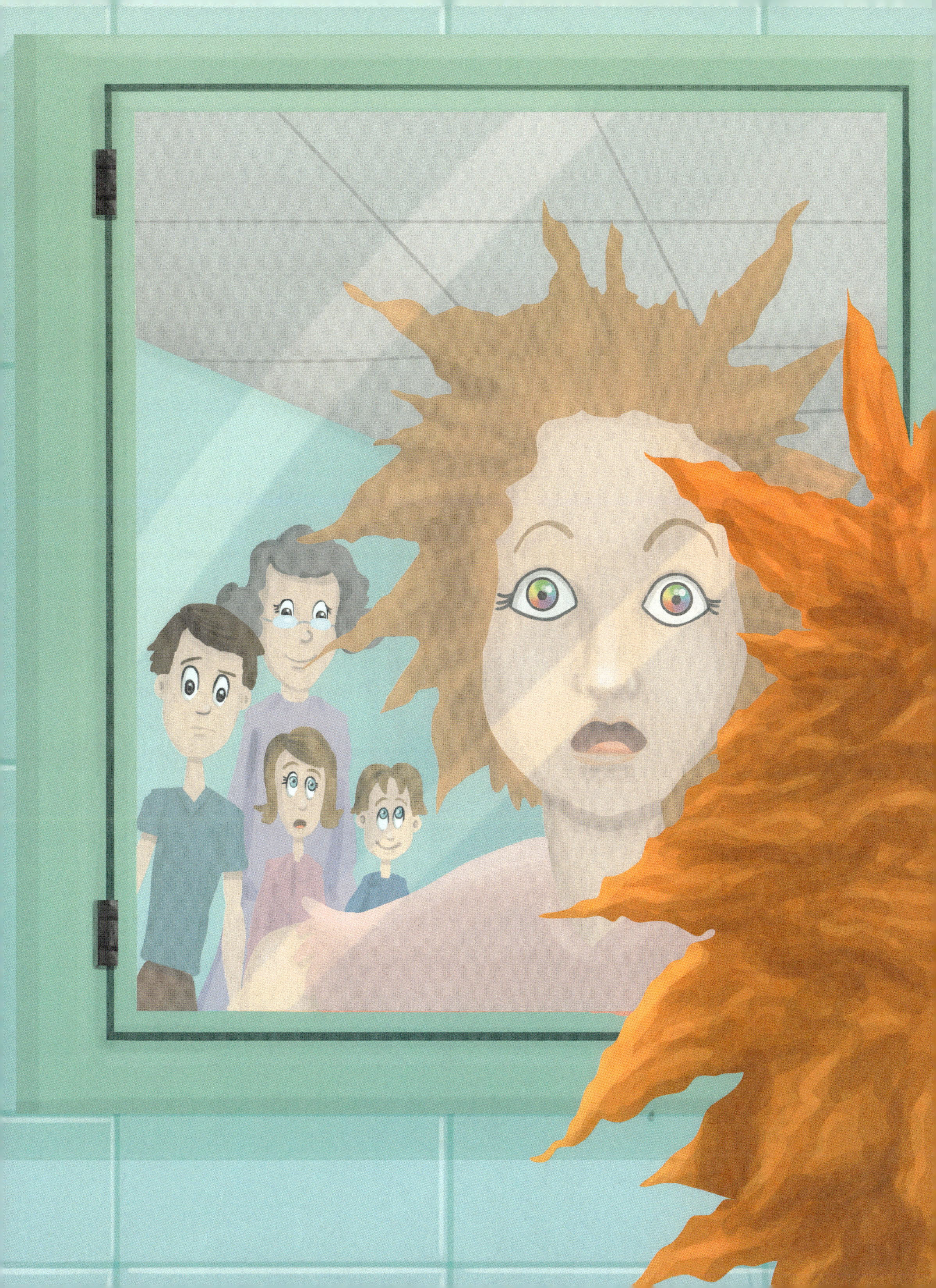

As the family continued to talk and try to figure out what Marie should do with her new body, a strange thing happened exactly sixty-three minutes after the shock took place.

"Mommm! You're shrinking back to your old self!" yelled Glen.

"I'm melting, I'm melting," called out Marie as she lowered to the ground.

"Oh no!" cried Angie as the family ran towards her.

"I'm just kidding." giggled Marie.

"Mommmmm!"

"Sorry, I've always wanted to say that." Her family shook their heads, but they had to admit it was pretty funny.

"This has to be the strangest thing I have seen." said Keith.

"I guess the electricity must have finally left my body. Luckily, otherwise I would have had to buy a whole new set of clothes!"

The family wished they had taken a few pictures because they were pretty sure no one was going to believe what had happened earlier that day.

Or would they?

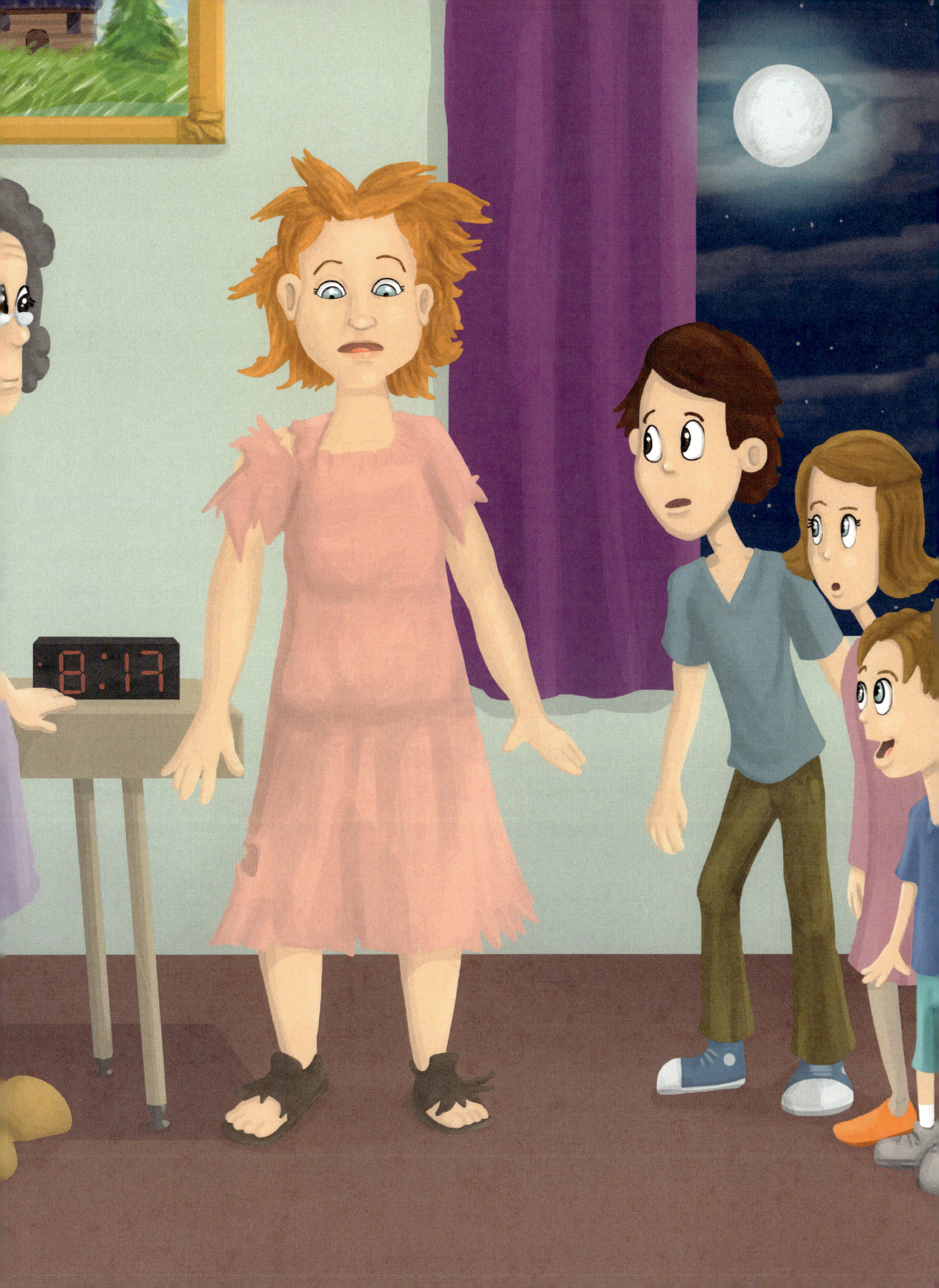
8:17

Later that night, as Marie was sitting down to read a bedtime story to her children, she began drinking another cup of her mom's homemade tea and ... the transformation started all over again!

"This doesn't make any sense!" Marie looked out the window to see if another storm had begun.

"Mom, I've got it! I think it's the electricity still in your body along with granny's homemade tea that makes all those changes," concluded Keith proudly.

Well, this is how this shocking event started, the beginning of her-story, and how a super mom became Supermom. Marie and her family decided that night that her 'new-found' powers should be used for good deeds to help others in their community. They came up with an idea for her superhero name and a clever disguise to keep her true identity a secret. Soon after they discovered the reasons behind her eyes turning rainbow colour and sudden interest in building things.

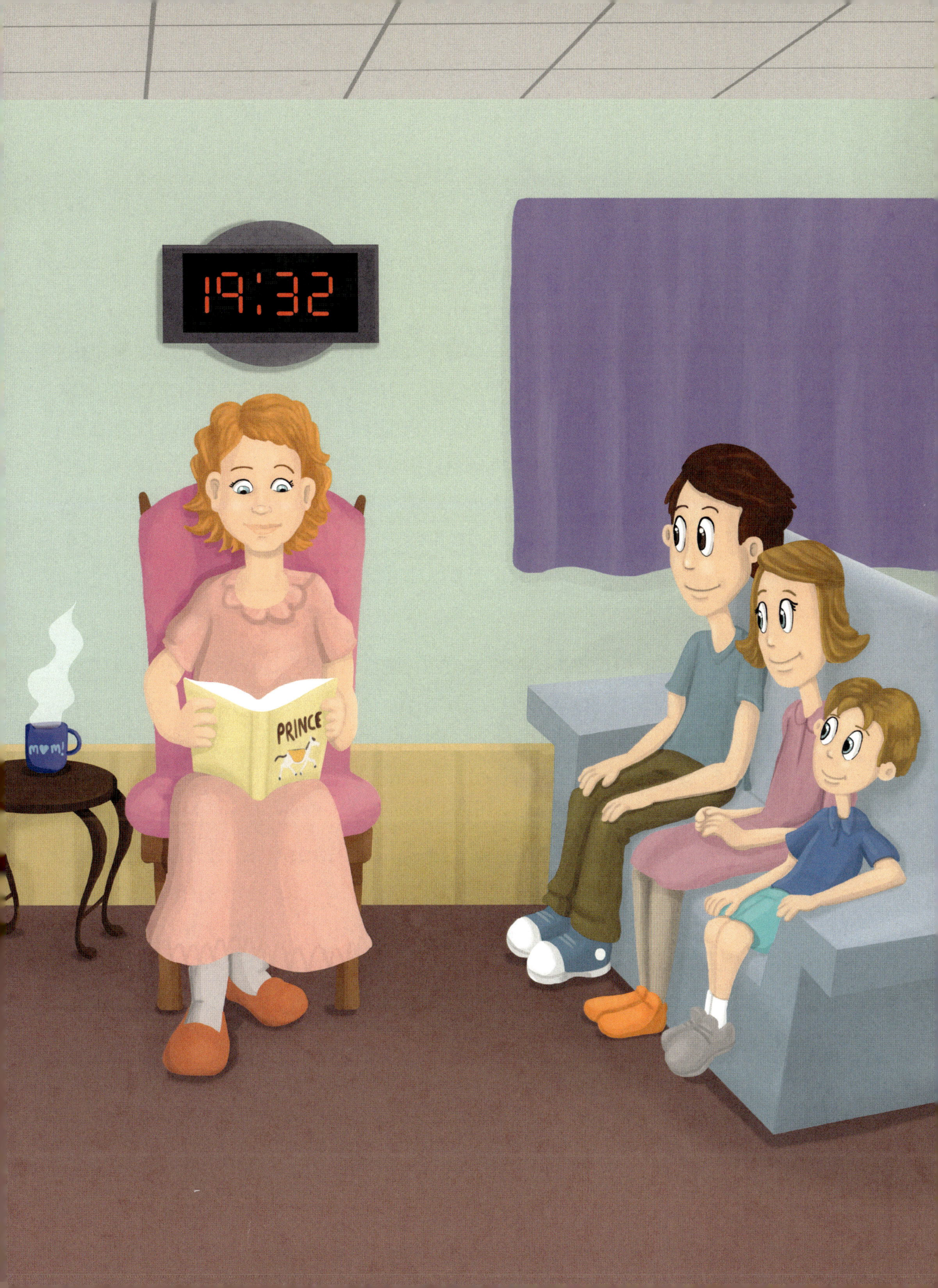
19:32
PRINCE
mom!

It was not long before word got around that there was a superhero living in the community. Whenever anyone needed her help, they would shout out, "SUPERMOM!" Marie would speak with them on her special ring. After taking a quick drink of grandma's tea, she would run into the nearest closet and change into her disguise in just two seconds! She wore a purple cape and mask, curlers in her hair, an 'I mean business' pink outfit, which included a special Supermom emblem designed by her kids, and a pair of comfortable steel toe boots.

Her rainbow-coloured eyes provided her with the ability to temporarily hypnotize both people and animals. Supermom could turn naughty kids into nice kids, in fact, she could even make them eat all their vegetables. The freak accident also turned Marie into a M.O.M. - a Mastermind of Mechanics. She could take common household items and change them into a special type of gadget: blender defender, dryer crier, mop cop, and much, much more. Her feather duster buster could make people or things move with a quick flick of her wrist.

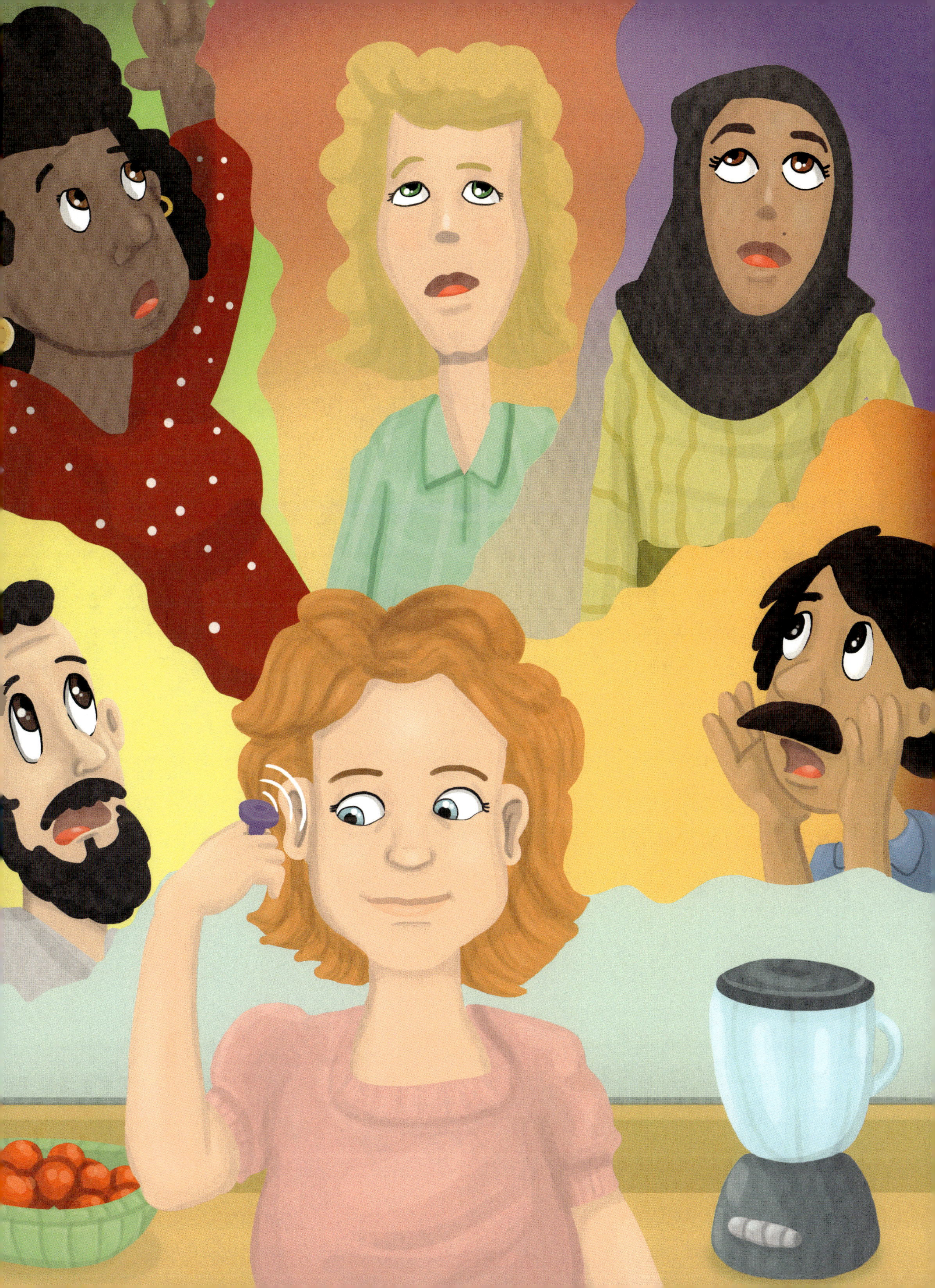

One night while Marie was working on an electric kettle, she received a desperate call for help on her 'care-ring'.

"Yes. Okay. Oh my. That is not nice at all. You're kidding!"

It was a mom whose twins were messing up their room with last week's garbage!

"No problem at all. I will be there in less than a minute," she replied and winked to her family to let them know that her help was needed.

She took a drink of her mom's special tea before quickly changing into her disguise. Marie kissed and hugged her family goodbye and then sped off to the twins' house on her trusty electric broom. When she arrived, she politely knocked on the door and waited patiently for someone to let her in.

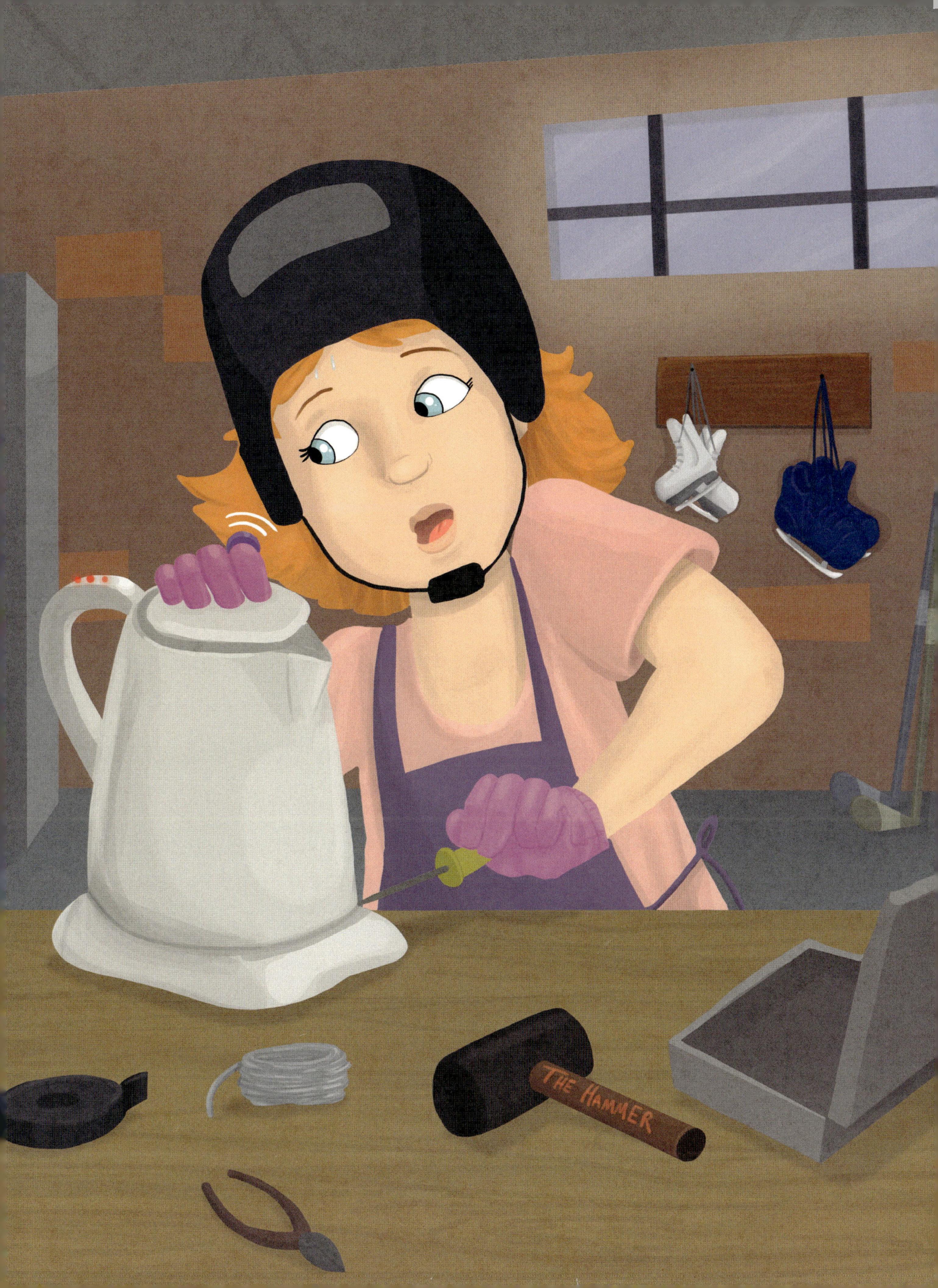
THE HAMMER

Inside the house, the twins were still up to no good as they searched for other things to toss about.

"Please, Cassy and Bella, stop messing up the house!" cried their mom in desperation.

"We're not messing it up. We just thought it could use a little decorating. Ha, ha, ha!" laughed Bella.

"Yeah, mommy. You are always telling us to use our imagination! Hee, hee, hee." Cassy responded sarcastically.

"Nice one, sis!" nodded Bella as she high-fived Cassy.

Supermom eventually picked the lock on the door with a bobby pin and entered the house holding her feather duster buster as she gave a quick wink and smile towards the mom.

* FLORIDA *
CANDY
CHOCOLATE
EVERYONE LOVES JOHNNY
CAMP IS LIFE
CANDY

The twins quickly stopped toilet papering the kitchen when they noticed Supermom, but then they whispered something to each other, followed by a look of great excitement.

"Who are you? Our new cleaning lady?" snickered Cassy.

Supermom confidently announced as she walked in front of the girls: "I am - Supermom, and it will be the two of you who will be cleaning up!"

"Sure, we will."

Bella giggled: "Aren't you a little too old to dress up for Halloween?"

"Very funny - I will be putting an end to your tricks with how you are treating your mom!"

The twins bolted towards Supermom and began wrapping her up with toilet paper, causing Supermom to drop her feather duster buster. Cassy picked it up and started to spin Supermom around in circles. Bella grabbed the feather duster buster and began to do the same to her mother.

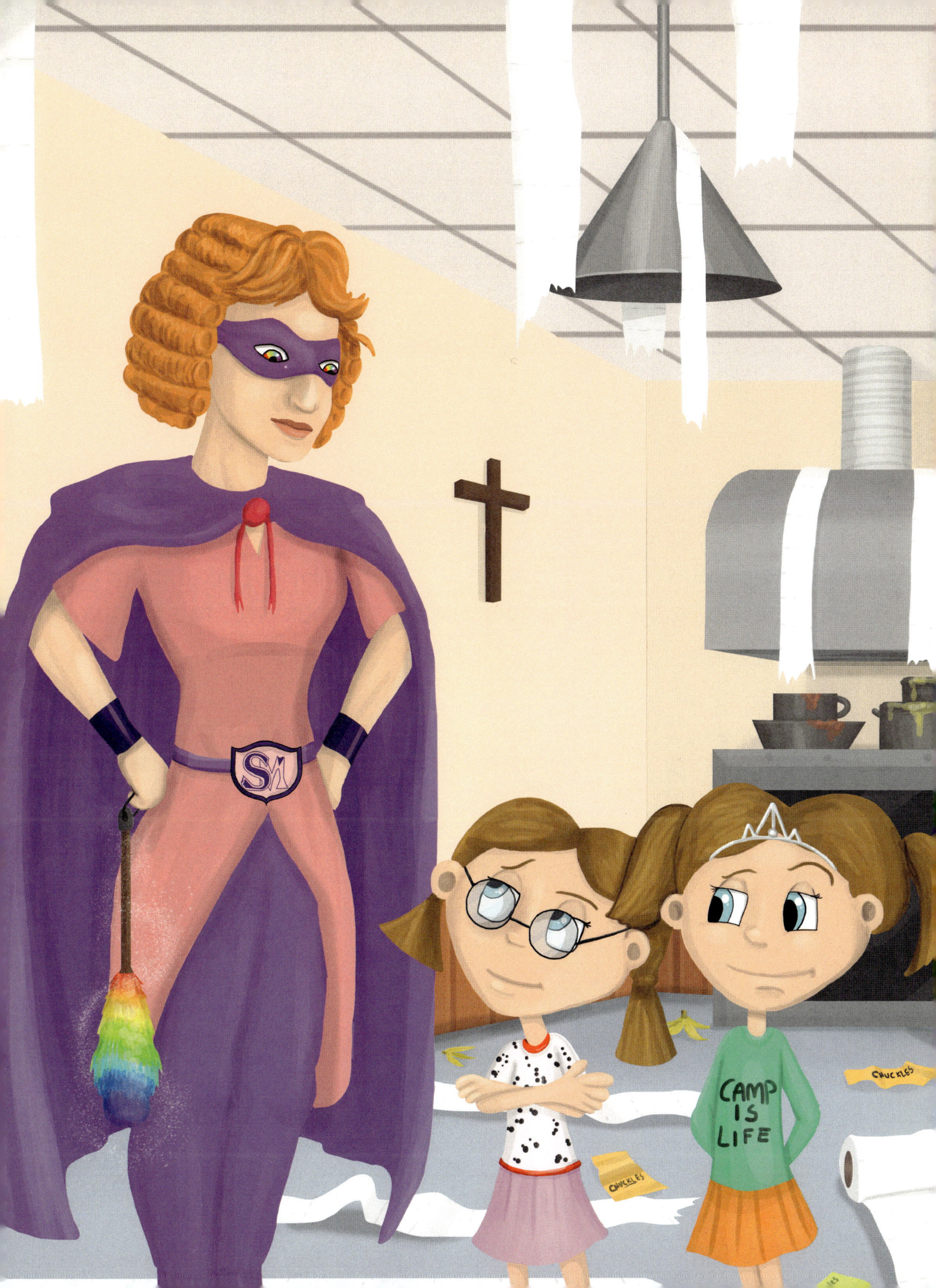
SM
CAMP IS LIFE
CHUCKLES
CHUCKLES

Supermom was able to regain her senses and hypnotized the twins with her powerful rainbow eyes. The children's mother couldn't believe what she was seeing. Her two daughters were cleaning up their room, and then they started to clean up the whole house!

"Must-clean-up-room. Must-change-cat's-litter-box. Must-put-a-way-our-dishes!" echoed the twins as they ran around the house and even swept up their cat, Baggy.

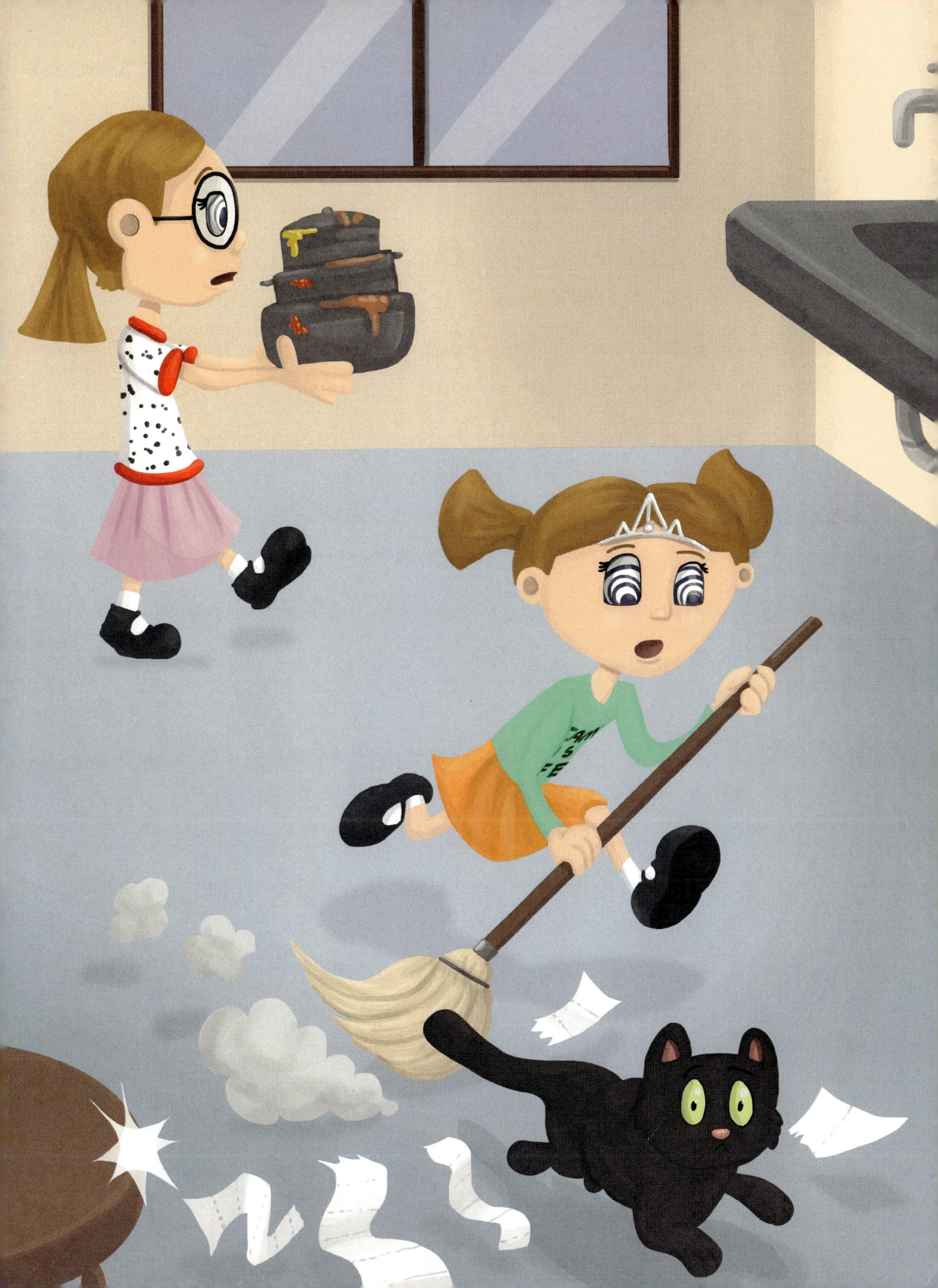

After the trance wore off, the twins realized how poorly they behaved and apologized to their mom.

"We're so sorry, mom. It's just you don't seem to pay any attention to us when we do good things," sobbed Cassy.

"I'm sorry too, girls. I promise to let you know how great of a job you are doing when you do help out," their mom said as she hugged both of her daughters.

"Perhaps the next time you want to be creative and use your imagination, you can treat your mom and neighbours to a super play!"

"Great idea!" Bella said as she and Cassy danced about.

"I got it! You should do one about clouds or snow!"

"Sure ... but mom why would you want us to do one about those things?" Cassy replied with a puzzled look.

"What else are we going to do with all this unrolled toilet paper?" joked their mom.

All four of them started to laugh as they looked at the big fluffy pile of toilet paper the twins had swept into the corner.

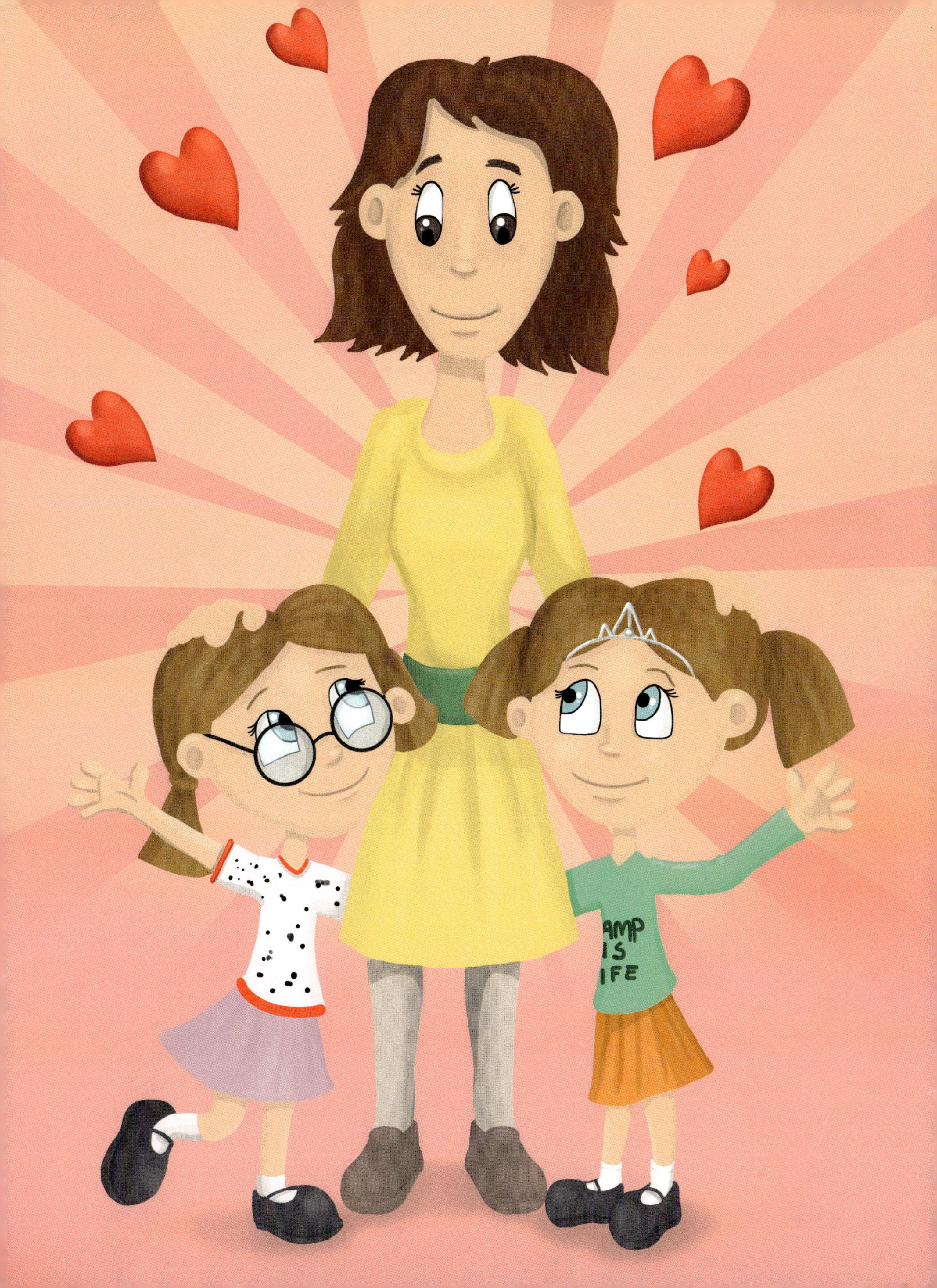

With a look of great satisfaction, and wiping a tear from her eye, Supermom said, "It sounds like the three of you have worked things out." She quickly slipped her feather duster buster into the mother's purse and whispered to her: "Just in case this happens again! Plus, it might come in handy when they become teenagers."

Supermom hugged the girls and their mom and then got ready to fly back to her own family. As she looked back to wave goodbye, she could see and hear the twins sing: "She's Supermom, yeah, yeah, yeah, she's Supermom! Flying through air, providing help, love, and care. She's Supermom, yeah, yeah, yeah, she's Supermom!"

When she got home, Marie told her family about everything that happened, and they were all so very proud of her.

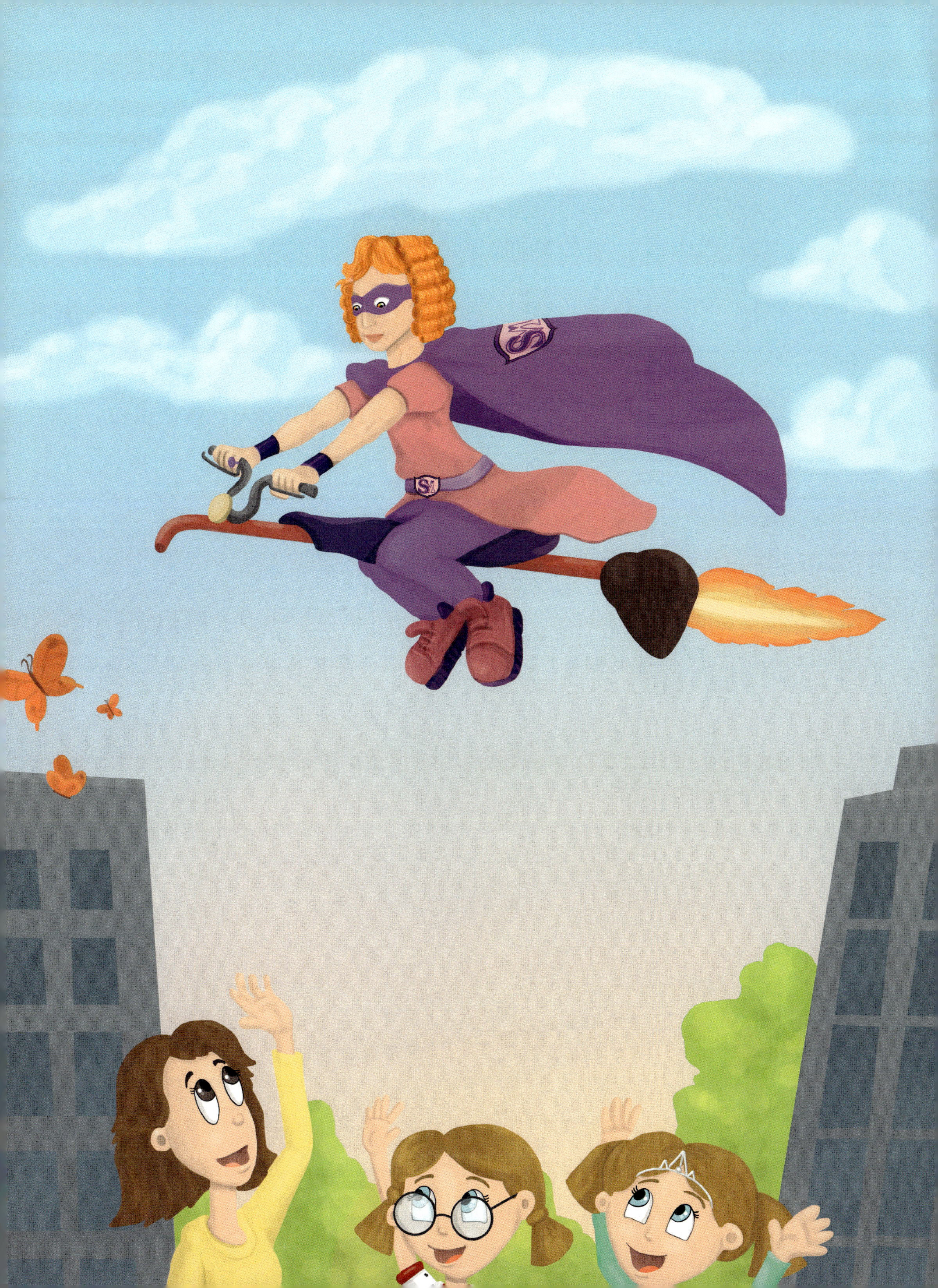

Stay tuned for more adventures as *Supermom* provides help, love, and care throughout her community.

"She's Supermom, yeah, yeah, yeah, she's Supermom! Flying through air, providing help, love, and care. She's Supermom, yeah, yeah, yeah, she's Supermom!"

Draw a picture below of you doing something super for your family or community. Don't forget to include your cape and costume!

I am a super kid!

Made in the USA
Monee, IL
20 May 2021